A Visit to the Farm

by Lara Bergen
illustrated by Dan Kanemoto

Simon Spotlight/Nick Jr.

New York   London   Toronto   Sydney   Singapore

Based on the TV series *Little Bill*® created by Bill Cosby as seen on Nick Jr.®

SIMON SPOTLIGHT
An imprint of Simon & Schuster Children's Publishing Division
1230 Avenue of the Americas, New York, New York 10020
Copyright © 2004 Viacom International Inc. All rights reserved.
NICKELODEON, NICK JR., and all related titles, logos, and characters are trademarks of
Viacom International Inc. *Little Bill* is a trademark of Smiley, Inc.
Manufactured in the United States of America
First Edition   10 9 8 7 6 5 4 3 2 1
ISBN 0-689-86269-5

Little Bill could hardly wait to get to school.

"Today Miss Murray is taking us to a farm!" he told his family.

Little Bill had never been to a farm before.

"I remember going there when I was in kindergarten," his brother,

Bobby, said. "My favorite part was the kids!"

Kids . . . thought Little Bill as he made his way to school. He was
hoping to see animals on the farm. But he imagined that a farm full of
kids would be fun too. . . .

"We're going to the farm today! We're going to the farm today!" Little Bill's friends, Andrew and Kiku, were chanting. And it didn't take long for Little Bill to join in too.

"That's right," Miss Murray told them. "So let's get ready, class. The bus will be here soon."

Little Bill loved riding on the bus with his classmates. He picked a seat next to his cousin Fuchsia. Everyone sang songs while Miss Murray passed around juice and cookies.

The time went by fast and soon Miss Murray called out, "We're here!"

Little Bill looked out the window. He could see several barns and lots of grassy fields full of cows and horses and sheep.

Oh, boy!, he thought.

Then a woman in overalls stepped onto the bus.

"Hi," she said. "My name is Liz. Welcome to my farm!"

"You're in luck," Farmer Liz told the class as she led them into a big barn. "We have lots of new baby animals on the farm this spring."

"Yeah! Baby animals!" the class cheered.

"First I'd like you to meet these brand-new brothers and sisters,"
Farmer Liz said, stopping in front of a pen.

Right away Little Bill and his friends ran to peek in.

"Meet Melody, the sow, and her ten newborn piglets," Farmer Liz said. "They're nursing right now."

Little Bill looked down at the mother pig giving her babies milk.

"Did you know that pigs are the smartest animals on the farm?" the farmer asked. "You can teach a pig to roll over and beg, just like a dog."

Then Farmer Liz led the class to a hutch made out of wire and wood.

"Baby bunnies!" Little Bill exclaimed. "Just like Wabbit's!"

"Wabbit is our classroom pet," Miss Murray explained. "She had babies not too long ago."

"Oh," said Farmer Liz, "so you know all about how baby rabbits are born with their eyes closed and no fur at all."

"Yep," said Little Bill. "It was hard to wait till they were big enough to hold!"

"Well, you can hold these babies," Farmer Liz told him. "They're already four weeks old. But be very gentle. And one at a time . . ."

The next thing Farmer Liz showed them was a box with a warm yellow lightbulb shining on it—and two tiny, wet-looking chicks inside.

"Did they just take a bath?" Fuchsia asked.

"No," said Farmer Liz. "They've just spent the last few hours hatching from their shells. It will take them a few more hours to get nice and fluffy."

"This calf is just a few hours old, too," Farmer Liz said. "She was born this morning!"

"And she's already standing up?" asked Little Bill.

"Oh, yes," said Farmer Liz. "She has to eat. Did you know her mother carried her for nine months, just like yours? Of course she weighs eighty pounds and you probably weighed eight."

Back outside, Farmer Liz led Little Bill's class up to some animals he had never seen before.

"These are our llamas," Farmer Liz told them. "They're great to have on the farm. They can carry things on their backs. Their hair makes wonderful, warm sweaters. And they're even good at guarding our sheep! The baby one is called a *cria*."

Monty turned to Little Bill. "There sure *are* a lot of babies on this farm," he said.

Little Bill agreed. But then Bobby's words came back to him . . . and Little Bill raised his hand.

"Where are your kids?" he asked Farmer Liz.

"I'm glad you asked!" she replied, smiling. "Follow me!"

Little Bill and his friends followed Farmer Liz to another grassy pasture.

"Here they are," she said proudly. "My newest kids!"

"Kids?" Little Bill spoke up. "But all I see are goats."

Farmer Liz smiled. "Baby goats are called kids," she explained. "Their mommies are called nannies, and their dads are called billy goats."

"Oh!" said Little Bill. He could see why they were Bobby's favorite. They were really cute. And they looked like they liked to play.

"Would you like to feed them?" Farmer Liz asked.

"YES!" the whole class cheered.

After feeding the kids it was time for Little Bill's class to head back to school in time for lunch themselves. But it was hard to say good-bye.

Little Bill offered a small, spotted kid his last pellet of food and gently rubbed its back.

"Little Billy's a good kid, isn't he?" asked Farmer Liz.

"Little *Billy*?!" said Little Bill.

"Mmm-hmm," Farmer Liz nodded.

"That's like my name!" said Little Bill.

He gave the kid another pat. "Hello, Little Billy," he whispered. "My name's Little Bill. Maybe I'll see you again one day, when we're both *Big* Bills!"

On the way home Fuchsia led the class in a round of "Farmer Liz Had a Farm."

Little Bill sang at the top of his lungs, *"And on her farm she had some kids! E-I-E-I-O!"*

It was the perfect way to end a perfect trip, Little Bill thought. And he couldn't wait to get home, so he could tell Bobby all about it!